The Face of Doom

Jack McAlpin raced his car through the pouring rain. He fought to keep his eyes on the highway past the swishing windshield wipers.

But he couldn't shake the feeling that there was something behind him. He felt it coming closer and closer, gaining ground with every turn of the tires.

Don't be nuts, he told himself as he glanced in the side view mirror. *Nothing's behind you.*

But the feeling was too strong. Like a magnet it drew his gaze to the rearview mirror.

His eyes bulged in shock at what they saw.

Staring back at him was a face with its skin bloody and rotting, sections of bone peeking through . . .

Other X-Files books in this series

Voyager

THE(X)FILES™

Fresh Bones

Novelization by Les Martin

Based on the television series
The X-Files created by
Chris Carter

Based on the teleplay
written by Howard Gordon

HarperCollins*Publishers*

Voyager
An Imprint of HarperCollins*Publishers*
77–85 Fulham Palace Road,
Hammersmith, London W6 8JB

This paperback edition 1997
1 2 3 4 5 6 7 8 9

First published in the USA by HarperTrophy
A division of HarperCollins*Publishers* 1997

ISBN 0 00 648329 1

Set in Goudy

Printed and bound in Great Britain by
Caledonian International Book Manufacturing Ltd, Glasgow

To Janet, again and again
and again

Chapter One

It was the most horrible sound that a mother could hear.

A baby was crying.

Her baby.

Robin McAlpin woke with a start. She felt as though she had hardly closed her eyes since the last time the baby's wailing had shattered her sleep. She grunted drowsily. Still curled in a ball, her eyes glued shut, she raised her head from the pillow just enough to say, "Your turn to get his bottle, honey."

There was no answer. From the next room, the baby cried louder. From outside the bedroom window, rolling thunder threatened a storm.

"Jack?" Robin said a little louder, her eyelids still too heavy to open.

Again there was no answer from her husband's side of the bed.

Robin's body stiffened. Her eyes shot open. She turned her head and saw that she was alone in the bed.

Then she heard another sound.

It came from behind the closed door of the bathroom.

She knew what it was, and it made her wince even more than the baby's crying.

She could picture her husband bent over the toilet bowl. She could hear him vomiting up his dinner from the evening before. And maybe his lunch as well.

She slid out from between the sheets and padded across the bedroom to the bathroom. As she neared the door, the toilet flushed.

"Honey?" Robin said through the door. Her voice was soothing. It was the voice she used when the baby was upset. "You still feeling sick?"

She heard the door handle turning. She stepped aside as the door swung open and Jack strode angrily out.

Robin knew better than to get in Jack's

way. He was a six-footer who played fullback for his Marine Corps company's football team, and he looked it. The chest of his military-issue T-shirt bulged, and his biceps stretched the short sleeves.

Not that Jack's violent, Robin thought, even as she edged away. The man she had fallen in love with and married might be strong as a bull, but he was gentle as a lamb.

At least he used to be.

Right now his face was as dark as the early morning thunderclouds outside.

"What's the matter with you?" he growled, as he stormed past his wife. "Can't you hear the baby crying?"

Without looking at Robin, he went to the clothes rack and started putting on his Marine duty fatigues. Their camouflage pattern used to make Robin smile. They made Jack look like he was going off to a jungle war zone instead of duty at Folkstone, North Carolina. Robin no longer smiled when he put them on, though. Things just didn't seem funny anymore.

"Well, what are you waiting for?" Jack snapped, as he sat on the edge of the bed and pulled on his combat boots.

Robin sighed. She gave her husband a last glance. He did not answer her gaze but stayed sitting with his head bowed, even after he had tied the bootlaces.

Robin turned and went to the baby's room. The baby, at least, would accept her love.

Robin picked up the baby and rocked him in her arms. In just a few minutes he was gurgling happily.

She set him down and said, "Come on, Luke. Let's go into the kitchen and you can show Daddy what a big little man you are and how well you can walk and how nicely you can eat your breakfast."

At the mention of his father, little Luke's smile froze, then melted away.

Robin saw a look in her baby's eyes that she knew all too well.

It was the same look she desperately tried to hide when she looked at her husband.

It was fear.

Chapter Two

Jack McAlpin lost track of time as he sat staring down at his boots. Staring back at him was his face mirrored in the gleaming leather.

He finally forced his eyes away, but he couldn't get the image of his own face out of his head. It blotted out the face of his watch. He had to rub his eyes until they stung before he could focus on the time. He was late.

He gave his head a quick shake to snap himself out of his funk, then jumped to his feet and headed for the kitchen. He knew he should eat something before reporting for duty.

Robin managed a weak smile of welcome as her husband sat down wordlessly and grabbed a big box of dry cereal.

There had been a time when little Luke

would have laughed happily upon seeing his daddy. But his father had not played with him for weeks now. All Jack did lately was shout at Luke for anything he did or did not do.

What Luke did now was start crying.

"Can't you shut him up for a couple of minutes?" Jack barked as he poured the cereal into a bowl. "I don't need to hear a bawling kid first thing in the morning."

"Shhhh," Robin gentled the baby. Luke stopped crying but kept watching his daddy with wary eyes.

Jack didn't notice. His gaze zeroed in on the cereal bouncing into his bowl. When it was full, he put down the box. He poured in milk, grabbed a spoon, and dug in like a starving animal.

"You were having those awful dreams again last night," Robin said to him softly.

"I didn't sleep long enough to be dreaming," Jack answered, barely pausing as his jaws crunched away.

"I want you to see the doctor," Robin said. "Find out what's wrong."

Jack looked up from his food. Fury darkened his face. "I'll tell you what *I* want. I want to eat my breakfast in peace," he snarled. "You think that's possible?"

He turned back to his cereal, shoveled more into his mouth—and nearly choked as he looked into his bowl.

The bowl was filled with wormlike bugs, writhing and crawling over each other.

Maggots.

"Uggh," he said, spitting out everything left in his mouth. With the back of his hand, he tried to wipe the awful taste off his lips. Then his hand swept across the table, sending the bowl flying. It smashed to the floor, cereal and milk splashing out over the linoleum.

"Jack, what's wrong?" Robin asked. She was torn between concern for her husband and for her baby, who was now wailing in terror.

Her husband saved her the trouble of choosing. He stood up, knocking his chair over, and stomped out of the kitchen and out of the house.

There was a flash of lightning and a crack of thunder as he got into his car.

"That's all I need now—a storm to slow me down," he muttered as he started the car with a lurch. McAlpin knew that he couldn't afford to be late again. The colonel had been giving him a hard time recently. But with everything that had been going on—the nightmares, the nausea, and now this morning—it was getting harder and harder to act normal.

Jack raced his car through the pouring rain. He fought to keep his eyes on the highway past the swishing windshield wipers.

But he couldn't shake the feeling that there was something behind him. He felt it coming closer and closer, gaining ground with every turn of the tires.

Don't be nuts, he told himself, as he glanced in the side-view mirror. *Nothing's behind you.*

But the feeling grew too strong. Like a magnet it drew his gaze to the rearview mirror.

His eyes bulged in shock at what he saw.

Staring back at him was a face with its skin

bloody and rotting, sections of bone peeking through.

He could still recognize the face, though.

It was his face.

He could not stop staring at it.

And it would not go away.

There was only one thing to do.

His big fist hit the mirror, again and again and again.

Blood splattered from his knuckles as the mirror broke free from the windshield and clattered to the floor of the car. But McAlpin felt no pain. All he felt was the wild joy of destruction.

Then a sharp bounce of the car jolted him out of his frenzy.

The car had gone off the road and was speeding across an open field.

Suddenly filling the windshield was a huge oak tree.

That was the last thing he saw before everything plunged into darkness.

Chapter Three

The highway sign read: COUNTY ROAD 10. FOLKSTONE, NORTH CAROLINA.

"We're getting close to the crash site," said FBI Special Agent Fox Mulder, as the sign flashed by him. At the wheel of a rental car, he was pushing the speed limit on the empty blacktop. Beside him was his partner, Special Agent Dana Scully.

Scully passed him a photo from a thick file folder on her lap. The photo showed a handsome young man in Marine Corps dress uniform. He was beaming.

"His graduation from boot camp," Scully remarked. "He looks so full of hope for the future. Hard to think that his future's gone now."

Mulder gave the photo a glance and

handed it back. "Private John McAlpin. One of the few, the proud . . ." He let his voice trail off.

Out of the corner of his eye, Mulder saw Scully wince as she looked at another photo. He knew what the photo showed. He'd had a chance to go through the case file before Scully had arrived at FBI Headquarters in Washington earlier in the day. They had both been summoned there by beeper on their day off. Less than an hour later, they were on their way to North Carolina. Scully was using this final leg of the trip to fill herself in on the ugly details of the case.

"Private McAlpin was a model Marine— until last week," Mulder said, scanning the road for their destination. "A model Marine doesn't wrap his car around a tree."

Scully grimaced again as she gave the shot of the wreck a last look. Then she turned to a written report of the accident.

"Tests done on the body showed no trace of drugs or alcohol," she said. "And what was left of the car showed no evidence of brake, steering, or other mechanical failure."

"The military is calling it a suicide," Mulder said. "They're especially concerned because it's the second one in as many weeks."

"Both at the same base?" Scully asked.

"Yes," Mulder said. "Except that it's not exactly a base."

"What do you mean?" Scully asked.

"Flip to the back of the file and you'll see," said Mulder, keeping his eyes on the road ahead.

Scully did so. She found a photo of a long line of shabbily dressed black men, women, and children waiting to get their dinner. Also in the photo were Marines in combat fatigues. They were carrying weapons and keeping a close eye on the crowd.

"McAlpin belonged to a Marine detachment at the Folkstone Processing Center."

"Who was being processed?" Scully wanted to know.

"More than twelve thousand refugees waiting to get the word from Uncle Sam whether they can stay in this country," said Mulder.

"Folkstone . . . Folkstone . . . the name seems to ring a bell," Scully said. Her brow furrowed. "Wasn't there some kind of riot there about a month ago?"

Mulder nodded. His voice was grim: "A ten-year-old boy was killed—though the details of his death were never released."

"Messy," said Scully.

"Very," said Mulder. "The kind of mess that the military often prefers to sweep under the carpet."

"Then why did they contact us?" Scully asked.

"They didn't," said Mulder.

"Then who did?"

"Mrs. McAlpin called the FBI after the Marines refused her request to investigate her husband's death further," Mulder said.

"She doesn't think it was suicide?" Scully asked.

Mulder didn't answer. Instead he pulled the car over to the side of the road and stopped. He got out quickly, leaving Scully to scurry after him.

She caught up with him in front of a large, badly scarred tree. Above their heads, its twisted branches were black against the gray sky.

"This is the tree that stopped Private McAlpin's car," Mulder said. "We can see what there is to learn here."

"And what do you think a tree will tell us?" asked Scully.

"You never know what anything will tell you," said Mulder, as he slowly circled the tree. "Otherwise you wouldn't have to look."

Scully followed him, and stopped when she noticed Mulder staring at something.

"What on earth is that?" she wondered aloud.

Painted in white on the rough bark was a large circle. Within the circle was a cross dividing the circle into four parts. In each of the parts was a different symbol, none of which Scully recognized.

"State police reported that they found

'graffiti' on the bark," Mulder said. "But we can assume that this place is a little out of the way for a graffiti artist to be operating."

"It looks like some kind of primitive ritual symbol," said Scully. "But it's no religion or form of magic I know."

"Most of the refugees at Folkstone come from Haiti," said Mulder.

"Haiti?" Scully echoed. Then Mulder's meaning dawned. She shook her head and said, "You're not suggesting that voodoo is involved, are you? Because if you are, I think you've been watching too many old Hollywood movies, with blood sacrifices and zombies and the rest. You have to cut down on your late-night TV."

"We're here to investigate Mrs. McAlpin's suspicions," Mulder replied.

"She believes that voodoo is behind her husband's death?" Scully asked.

"She believes her husband didn't kill himself," said Mulder. "And she wants to know who did."

Chapter Four

The McAlpins lived in a modest house on a street lined with almost identical houses. But no two homes were exactly the same, just as no two families were exactly the same. Mulder and Scully checked out the McAlpin home before ringing the doorbell. Scully took out a miniature tape recorder, to record their observations.

"The house is in good repair," Mulder noted. "The windows are clean. The lawn is mowed. The flower garden in front is well tended. All this despite the fact that this most likely would not be a permanent residence. Military families such as the McAlpins have to make frequent moves—wherever duty calls."

Scully nodded, and added, "It gives evidence that the family believed it important to have a stable and satisfying home life—no matter what the pressures of the military."

Scully put the recorder back into her bag, and they rang the doorbell.

A woman in her twenties answered. She was quite pretty, with long blond hair and enormous brown eyes. But right now her hair was unkempt. And her eyes had an unfocused look, as if only a few blinks away from tears.

"Yes?" she said, looking at the visitors suspiciously.

"Mrs. Robin McAlpin?" Mulder asked.

"Yes."

"I'm Special Agent Mulder—and this is my partner, Special Agent Scully." He flashed his ID. Next to him, Scully did the same.

Robin McAlpin's face lit up. "You've come," she said, her voice filled with wonder. "I didn't think anyone would. I figured no one in authority would listen to me—not with the military saying I was crazy with grief. I mean, I admit that my ideas may seem weird, but . . ." She let her voice trail off, not wanting to cast doubt on her own story.

"Agent Scully and I specialize in cases that go beyond the boundaries of ordinary belief," Mulder assured her. "Now, if we could talk to you for a few minutes . . ."

Robin McAlpin opened the door wide. "What was I thinking, keeping you out here," she said. "Please come in."

She ushered them into the house.

"Mind if we go to the kitchen?" she said. "My little boy is playing there. I want to keep an eye on him."

On the kitchen floor, little Luke McAlpin was moving some toy soldiers around and making loud explosive sounds. After each "Bang!" he pushed over another one. He had enough troops to make the battle last a long time.

Robin shook her head. "Not even two years old—and he has the bug already," she said, her voice halfway between pride and regret. "I guess it's only natural. He worshiped his father. He used to love seeing Jack put on his uniform, until . . ." She paused, biting her lower lip, then sat down at the kitchen table.

Her elbows rested on the Formica tabletop, with her hands cradling her chin.

Mulder and Scully sat down too. Scully placed the recorder on the table between them.

"Do you mind if we tape your remarks, Mrs. McAlpin?" Scully asked.

Robin pulled herself together, raised her chin, and shook her head.

Scully snapped the recorder on and Mulder said, "You just used the word *until*, Mrs. McAlpin. Until what?"

"Until recently," Robin said. "Until Jack started acting . . . strange."

"Strange in what way?" Mulder asked.

"It's hard to describe," Robin said.

"Do the best you can."

"Well, Jack used to tell jokes," Robin began. Her eyes grew misty with memory. "They were pretty dumb, I guess. But the way he told them made me laugh. He was fun to be with. Then he got transferred to the camp. And the jokes stopped. Everything stopped. Nothing was very funny anymore."

"And this was only just when he started his current assignment?" Scully wanted to make sure.

"Yes," Robin said. "He was moody and tense. He never acted like that before."

"Did he ever discuss what went on in the camp?" Scully asked. "What his duties included?"

"No," Robin said, her voice bleak. "He'd just come home angry. Angrier and angrier, day after day. Mostly at himself. But sometimes he'd turn it on Luke and me."

Scully leaned forward. "Was he ever treated for stress or depression?"

Robin shook her head. "I tried getting him to talk to someone—even our minister. But Jack believed in dealing with his own problems. He was a sweet man, a good man, a kind man. But he did have this stubborn streak. He was a Marine."

"Did he believe in voodoo?" Mulder asked suddenly and sharply.

Robin had to smile at the idea. "Jack

believed in the Marines, his family, and football," she said. "That pretty much sums up everything he believed in."

"Then why and when did you first think that your husband's death might involve something . . . out of the ordinary?" Mulder asked.

Robin shifted·uncomfortably in her seat. "Look, I warned you that this all sounds weird. It's not the kind of thing I would normally suggest."

"As I told you, that does not trouble us," Mulder replied.

"One of the boys in Jack's squad told me what they found at the accident," Robin said hesitantly. "That strange mark on the tree. He said it was some kind of voodoo curse. They found the same mark on the stool that the Puerto Rican guy in the squad used to hang himself. Another so-called suicide."

"What is the name of the soldier who told you this?" Mulder asked.

"Harry Dunham," Robin said. "He's from

New Orleans. They have a lot of strange old beliefs down there. So he's pretty superstitious about that sort of thing."

"But you're not?" Mulder said.

Robin shook her head. "I never was. Besides, I was too shaken up by Jack dying to pay much attention to the story. I didn't really give it any thought, until . . ." She paused. She found it hard to say what came next.

"Until?" Mulder gently prodded.

Robin's face looked ready to dissolve. "Until Luke dug this up out of his sandbox."

Robin opened a paper bag that was sitting on the table. She pulled out a large conch shell and handed it to Mulder.

Mulder turned it over. Painted in red on its milky white interior was a symbol. The same symbol as on the tree where McAlpin had crashed.

"I know it sounds crazy, worrying about this," said Robin, her voice quivering. "But the truth is, I'm scared. I'm scared for my child. I don't know what to do anymore. Please, tell me I don't have to worry."

"We'll go to the camp and find out everything we can," Mulder promised.

Chapter Five

"The government didn't waste any money on appearances," Scully said when she got her first look at the Folkstone Immigration and Naturalization Service Processing Center.

She stood with Mulder in front of a high chain-link fence topped with razor wire. Through the fence she saw a yard crowded with men, women, and children. Most of them were wrapped in blankets to keep warm.

"The authorities had to get this place up and running fast," Mulder said. "The refugees came in a sudden flood when order broke down in Haiti. Plus Congress had just slashed the budget for construction. You can understand why they picked such an isolated spot. You don't have to worry about looks when there's no one to see."

Scully squinted at the large, run-down buildings beyond the yard. "Looks like they used old warehouses already here."

Mulder shrugged. "Warehousing goods. Warehousing people. Not much difference—unless you're one of the people."

At the front gate, an armed Marine in combat gear checked their IDs. His eyes went from their photos to their faces a couple of times each before he let them in. Even then, he didn't look very pleased to be doing so.

"He seemed as interested in keeping people out as keeping people in," Scully remarked when they were past him.

"I can see why those in charge might not be eager to have visitors," Mulder said, looking around him.

From outside, the crowded yard had seemed squalid. Inside the fence, it looked and smelled even worse.

Clearly there weren't many washing facilities available. The gray blankets and brightly hued clothes of the people were grimy, and so were their faces.

The looks on those faces told an even bleaker story. Though some younger men were playing soccer, and older ones were playing chess or cards or reading, and a few women were sewing or tending babies, most of the faces showed deadening boredom. Either that, or smoldering anger.

The armed Marines in the yard did not act bored. They were very much on the alert, as they kept close watch on the shuffling crowd.

"Where can we find your commanding officer?" Mulder asked one of the guards.

The Marine motioned with his semiautomatic rifle toward the largest of the buildings. "Colonel Wharton? In there. His office is up the stairs at the very back."

Dim light from weak bulbs and dirty windows lit the inside of the warehouse. People sat packed on slat benches at crude wooden tables, spooning food from chipped bowls. Part of the vast room had been sectioned off with hanging sheets to form makeshift sleeping quarters.

They were headed down an aisle between the sheets when a man built like a heavy-weight contender stepped in front of Scully.

Glowering, he grabbed her by the shoulders.

"*Pas remass li!*" he snarled. "*Un vas entrave si—ou remass li!*"

Scully didn't understand a word. She only knew that he spoke Creole. Like a spicy stew, the language was a blend of tongues from the native Haitians, the French who ruled Haiti for a time, and the Africans they brought over as slaves.

Whatever he was saying, though, the rage in his voice was clear. So was the pain of his tight grip on her shoulders.

Suddenly, before Mulder could step in, the pain went away.

A thin boy less than half the man's size gave him a hard shove.

The boy's voice wasn't loud, but it was cutting as he gave the man a Creole tongue-lashing.

Growling, the man moved away and van-ished around the corner of the aisle.

The boy watched him go, then turned back to Scully and Mulder.

"He is crazy," he said, flashing a wide smile. "He drink too much rum."

Then he concentrated on Scully. "Such a pretty lady," he said. "It's dangerous here. You need something *pour vous gardez*. I mean, to guard yourself. A charm. For protection."

The boy had somehow obtained a Marine combat vest, which hung loose on his thin frame. From it he pulled a faded cloth charm, less than six inches long, without arms or legs, and stuffed with a scented spice that Scully could not name.

Scully was not a person who believed in magic, much less charms.

But before she could tell the boy that, Mulder asked, "How much?"

Instantly the boy's gaze homed in on Mulder.

"Ten," the boy said, holding out his empty hand.

"Come on, Mulder," Scully said impatiently.

"Five," said Mulder, pulling a bill from his wallet.

Beaming, the boy grabbed the bill and handed Mulder the charm.

A moment later he was gone, leaving Mulder to pocket his purchase.

"Mulder—" Scully started to say.

"Hey," said Mulder. "You should always carry protection."

He took one more look at the scene around them before they headed up the stairs to the colonel's office.

Everywhere, eyes were turned on them.

Nowhere was there a friendly gaze.

"You never know what might happen," Mulder said.

Scully shrugged. "Well, that's why we're here. To find out."

Chapter Six

Colonel Samuel Wharton got to his feet when his orderly ushered Mulder and Scully into his office. Though a big man, he moved as quickly as a cat. He still had muscle, as rock hard as his shaven bald head. He looked combat-ready in his camouflage fatigues.

He came out from behind his gray metal desk and checked Mulder and Scully's IDs. Then he motioned for the two FBI agents to sit down. He, however, remained standing. He was clearly most comfortable looking down at people.

"I received a phone call from the bureau that you were coming," he said. "But I'm still not clear on what you're investigating here."

"Two of your men have died in two weeks—

supposedly of self-inflicted injuries," Mulder said.

"And I've taken every measure to see that it doesn't happen again," the colonel replied. "I've even flown in the 528th Combat Stress Control Detachment from Camp Lejeune."

Scully lifted her eyebrows. "But your soldiers aren't in combat," she said.

"In many ways, what we're dealing with here is worse," Wharton said. His voice was bitter.

"How so?" Scully asked.

"We're soldiers, not prison guards," Wharton said. "Here we're being asked to police a hostile population of foreigners without the resources to properly house or feed them. There are bound to be certain . . . conflicts. Conflicts that can explode as violently as anything you run into in war."

The colonel paused and shook his head grimly. "Except, of course, it isn't war—not war as we know it. Which means we cannot respond in the same way we would in war. Our hands are tied. And that produces a frustration more stressful than anything in combat."

"The refugees must be frustrated as well," Scully said. "They are not able to enter this country or go back to their own. I can only assume that your men bear the brunt of the refugees' frustration."

"It's hatred, pure and simple," Wharton said flatly. "They hate us. All I can do is see that they're processed as efficiently as possible. When we get them all sorted out, we can decide what to do with them. It's the only way to end this nightmare situation."

Before Scully could ask more questions, Mulder cut in. "Colonel Wharton, a certain ritualistic symbol was found at the scene of both deaths. What can you tell us about it?"

Wharton shrugged casually. "Not much," he said. "Apparently it's some kind of voodoo marking."

"Then I take it you haven't investigated it as a possibility," Mulder said.

"Possibility of what?" asked Wharton.

Mulder didn't have to say a word. His silence said it all.

Wharton's mouth curved in contempt. "You mean, you think voodoo killed those two men? Let's be serious, Agent Mulder. The only power voodoo has is to inflame the ignorant. All I've ever seen it do was cause a riot in my camp. One night they held some secret ceremony. The next day, all hell broke loose."

"We understand that one of the refugees was killed," said Mulder. "A young boy."

"And no one felt that tragedy more deeply than I," he said with sorrow. "Fortunately, I was able to identify the person responsible for starting the trouble."

"Who would that be?" asked Mulder.

"His name is Bauvais," the colonel said with contempt. "Pierre Bauvais. He claims to be some kind of revolutionary leader. He keeps trying to get the people here to be his followers. But he can forget about that now. Nobody is going to follow him into the isolation cell he's in."

"Could we speak to him?" Mulder asked.

"Sure, if you have a strong stomach for hogwash," Wharton said. "He can bend your ear for hours with his complaints about us and his claims about himself."

"I'll keep that in mind," Mulder said.

"Then be my guest," the colonel told him.

Mulder and Scully got to their feet. But before they left, Scully said, "I'd also like to examine Private McAlpin's body. I have a signed consent from his wife."

The colonel gave her a hard look. "One thing I'll say, you G-men—I mean, you G-*people*—are gluttons for punishment. But okay, you can have the pleasure of checking out the corpse. But I warn you, Agent Scully, it won't be a pretty sight. I'd hate to have you . . . upset."

Wharton paused for a moment, and then gestured toward the Marine standing at attention by the door. "Private Dunham will help you both with whatever you need," he said.

At the sound of the name "Dunham," Mulder and Scully exchanged quick glances.

They both remembered that name coming from Robin McAlpin.

He was the boy from New Orleans.

The boy who had talked about voodoo.

For the first time, they both gave the Marine who had ushered them in a close look.

His face was a blank mask.

But fear shone through in his eyes.

Chapter Seven

Death did not bother Captain Peter Foyle. The Marine doctor's voice was matter-of-fact, close to bored, as he told Scully, "The cause of Private McAlpin's death is no mystery. The boy was doing sixty when his car hit the tree."

Scully was with Captain Foyle in the camp morgue. Private Dunham had dropped her off there before taking Mulder to see the prisoner Bauvais. Scully had her job to do, Mulder had his.

Scully's voice was as businesslike as Captain Foyle's as she pursued her inquiry. "So you pronounced him dead at the scene?"

"It took only a few minutes," Foyle said.

"And afterward, did you investigate the cause of death?" Scully asked.

Captain Foyle smiled at that—a thin smile.

"His head was hanging from his neck like a broken flower," Foyle said. "He was not breathing. His heart was not beating. I saw no reason to conduct an autopsy. And I still don't."

Foyle must have seen a glimmer of doubt in Scully's eyes.

"You can take a look and decide for yourself," he said. He led her to a wall lined with towering racks of large sliding stainless steel drawers.

Foyle paused in front of a drawer. The name taped on it was MCALPIN, JOHN J.

"As you will see, there is absolutely nothing mysterious about Private McAlpin's demise," he said as he slid the large drawer open.

"What the—?" he shouted.

Inside the drawer was a dead dog. The corpse was stiff with rigor mortis. Its legs were extended as if stopped in the midst of a leap. Its jaws were open, fangs gleaming in a frozen snarl.

Scully leaned forward for a closer look.

"Dead without a doubt," she said. "Do you plan to do an autopsy, Captain Foyle? I'd be glad to help. Perhaps it was rabies. Or a rare tropical disease. Unless it's one of your canine corps."

Captain Foyle wasn't in the mood for jokes. "What kind of sick prank is this?" he roared. Then he turned and gave an earsplitting shout to the next room. "Private Jackson, in here on the double! Who the devil has been playing games?"

Private Jackson's face was pale with dread as he came running to answer the captain's call.

But it wasn't as pale as Private Dunham's face as he led Mulder to Pierre Bauvais's cell. Dunham's military mask had started dissolving the moment they'd left the colonel's office. By now the private looked very young and very scared.

They were moving through an underground corridor, their footsteps echoing in the silence.

The corridor was lined with wire mesh enclosures, some empty, a few with prisoners in them.

"They look like animal cages," Mulder remarked.

"They were put up in a hurry," Dunham answered. "Anyway, they do their job. Nobody gets out of them."

Dunham spoke without turning his head. He clearly did not want to meet Mulder's eye.

After a few more steps, Mulder broke the growing silence. "You're Harry Dunham, right?"

"Yes sir." Dunham forced the words out, his eyes still straight ahead.

"You knew Private McAlpin, am I correct?" Mulder asked.

Dunham opened his mouth, then closed it again. Mulder could see his Adam's apple bobbing as the young Marine swallowed hard.

"His wife said you two were friends," Mulder prompted him.

"We were in the same squad," Dunham said.

"Do you have any idea why McAlpin might have taken his own life?"

"I can't say, sir."

"You can't or you won't?" Mulder demanded.

"We're here, sir," Dunham said with relief.

They had reached the last cage in the line. Dunham put a key in the lock on the heavy mesh door. Before he turned it, he asked, "Do you want me to come in with you?"

"I'd prefer to be alone with Bauvais," Mulder told him.

"Yes sir," Dunham said. "But I warn you, this man has been known to be violent."

"Thanks for the warning," Mulder said.

"In any event, I'll keep in listening range if you need help," Dunham said.

"I'd prefer that my conversation with him be private," Mulder said.

"In shouting range then," Dunham said.

"Thank you," Mulder said. "I hope that won't be necessary."

Dunham cast a look at the large figure of a man sitting on his bunk in semidarkness.

"I hope so too, sir," he said, as he swung open the door, let Mulder in, and locked it behind him.

Chapter Eight

Pierre Bauvais was built strong as steel—but his eyes were more powerful still. Even darker than his skin, they burned like the sun burning through mist.

Those eyes fixed on Mulder as he said, "My name is Mulder. I'm with the FBI."

Bauvais gave Mulder a wry smile of welcome, though it must have been painful. Mulder could see a scab on the prisoner's lip where it had been split.

"Yes, Mr. FBI Man?" Bauvais responded, staying seated on his bunk. His English was clear, though he spoke with an island lilt.

"I'm hoping you can answer some questions," Mulder said.

"About what?" Bauvais asked, but with not even a trace of curiosity.

Mulder had an idea that Bauvais knew exactly what was coming next.

"About the two U.S. Marines who took their own lives," Mulder said.

Bauvais shook his head. "It is a terrible shame," he said, and he seemed to mean it.

"I'm not convinced it was that simple," Mulder told him.

The prisoner gave another painful smile. "You don't by any chance think I was involved, do you?" he asked.

When Mulder did not answer, Bauvais went on. "How could I have been—when they keep me locked in here?"

"You tell me," Mulder said.

Mulder took three photos from his jacket and handed them to Bauvais, who looked at them one by one.

"And what can I tell you about these?" the prisoner asked.

"These photos were taken at the sites of both deaths," Mulder said. "One is of the tree that a Marine's car hit. One is a stool that another Marine stood on before hanging himself. And the third is a conch shell found buried the yard of one of the dead Marines' homes."

"Yes?" Bauvais responded. "And so?"

"As you can see," Mulder continued, "the same painted symbol appears in all photos."

"Yes, I see," said Bauvais, still not making any comment.

"Can you tell me what that symbol is?" Mulder asked.

"Why? What do you expect to learn from this?"

"Just the truth," Mulder said flatly. "One of the dead men left behind a wife and a young son. His wife is too frightened even to mourn. She deserves some peace of mind. I'm sure, as a human being, you can understand that."

Bauvais stood up to stand face to face with Mulder. Looking into Mulder's eyes, he said, "This symbol, it is Haitian. We call it *locomiroir*."

"And what does it mean?" Mulder asked.

"It stands for the crossroads between the two worlds—the world of the living and the world beyond life." Bauvais's voice took on the rhythm of a chant. "It is the mirror into which each man must look someday, the mirror in which a man must confront his true self."

Bauvais paused to let his meaning sink in. When he spoke again, his voice was different, dry and mocking. "Those two Marines— maybe they did not like what they saw."

Bauvais handed the photos back to Mulder. He clearly had said all he was going to on the subject.

Mulder tried a different tack. "Colonel Wharton claims you incited the riot here last month."

Bauvais did not shake his head in denial. Instead his chin rose proudly.

"Do you know the history of my country?" Bauvais demanded.

"Probably not as well as I should," Mulder said.

"Haiti was born when slaves rose up against their French masters and defeated the finest army Napoleon could send to crush them," Bauvais said. "Freedom is our most sacred legacy. And in the end, no military force will keep us from claiming it—not even the U.S. Marines."

"Then you'd kill to win your freedom?" Mulder asked.

For the first time, anger entered the prisoner's voice. "Wharton won't let us return home. That's all we want."

"But I thought—" Mulder said.

"We came here fleeing for our lives," Bauvais said. "But now the time of terror in Haiti is over. We want to return to build a new nation."

Before Mulder could ask anything more, a voice came from outside the cage.

"Mulder, I need to talk to you," Scully said.

Beside her, Dunham opened the cage door, and she came rushing in.

But before she could speak, Bauvais said, "She's come to tell you—the Marine is gone."

Open-mouthed, Scully turned to him. "How did you know?"

Bauvais smiled. "I am good at guessing things. You know, native intuition." Then his smile faded as he said, "The gods have warned you."

"What happened, Scully?" Mulder wanted to know.

"Someone stole McAlpin's body," Scully told him. "Replaced it with what seems to be the corpse of dog."

"They will only warn you once," Bauvais told Scully. Then he gave a chill warning of his own. "After that—no magic will save you."

Chapter Nine

It was night, and a fine rain was falling when Mulder and Scully drove away from the camp. The headlights cut through the drizzle to shine on the blacktop as Mulder and Scully talked over the case, trying to find their way through the darkening mystery.

"Somehow, Bauvais must have switched the bodies," Scully maintained. She was at the wheel and had to speak loudly over the sound of the windshield wipers.

"That would have been quite a trick," Mulder countered. "Considering Bauvais has been locked up in isolation for the last month."

"Then he had someone else do it," Scully said. "We know he's a kind of leader in the camp. He must have followers. And there's usually a way for prisoners to communicate with the outside world. That sort of thing happens in even in the best-run prisons. It could certainly happen here."

"True enough," Mulder said. "But on the other hand, you could find no evidence of anyone breaking into the morgue. And the officer in charge assured you that the security there was impossible to breach."

"Captain Foyle strongly indicated that," Scully acknowledged. "It seems that despite Colonel Wharton's doubts, the men under him take the talk about voodoo quite seriously. They don't know much about it, but they do know that corpses play a big part in it."

"They must have seen the same old Hollywood movies you warned me about," said Mulder. "The ones that featured zombies—the living dead."

"It is a distinct possibility," Scully said. "In any event, the soldiers on morgue detail guard the place as if it were Fort Knox."

"After this incident, I'm afraid, those fears of voodoo activity will be stronger than ever," Mulder said, looking out at the night and the rain. Not turning his head, he said to Scully, "We, of course, know better, don't we?"

"Mulder, what I know for sure is that whoever stole the corpse was very thorough and very clever," Scully declared. "I don't accept the possibility that it was the work of voodoo or any other kind of spirit or form of magic."

Mulder knew Scully better than to try to argue. He merely reached into his pocket and pulled out the cloth charm the boy in the camp had sold him. Scully grimaced when she saw it.

"Just in case," Mulder said. "I believe in covering my bases." Attached to the charm were strings that would allow a person to wear it around the wrist or neck. He used them to hang it on the rearview mirror.

"Mulder," Scully said, "the only power that voodoo has comes through instilling fear in people. You saw how Bauvais tried to shake me up—with information he doubtless got through the prison grapevine. I must admit, it almost worked. The power of suggestion is considerable. Fortunately, so is the power of reason—and I've had time to think things through."

Scully reached out and gave the hanging charm a flick of her finger. "This is no more magic than a pair of fuzzy dice," she said.

She would have said more if Mulder hadn't suddenly shouted, "*Scully, watch out!*"

Scully looked at the road and saw the large, blurred figure of a man directly in front of the car—and a flash of a face staring blankly into the headlights. She swung the steering wheel violently to the right, jamming on the brakes as she did so.

The moment the car skidded to a stop at the side of the road, Scully and Mulder jumped out and ran toward the man who was now staggering down the road.

The car's headlights were still on. Their beams shone on the man's broad back. He wore a dark olive T-shirt, camouflage fatigue pants, and combat boots. He was lurching and stumbling, as if he were sleepwalking through a nightmare.

Mulder caught up with him first.

"Hey," Mulder shouted, grabbed the big man by the shoulder, and turned him around.

He did not resist. He turned as easily as a top and stood facing them.

He had once been good looking. But now his face was marked by ugly, bloody wounds on the forehead, the nose, the cheeks, the chin.

His eyes stared sightlessly at Mulder and Scully.

Mulder reached out for the dog tag that dangled from the man's neck. He pulled it close enough to read it.

Scully's eyes opened wide as she read the name over Mulder's shoulder.

"Private McAlpin?" she asked.

Chapter Ten

Colonel Wharton's stress team had set up a special ward in the camp hospital for patients with mental and emotional illnesses.

Right now Private Jack McAlpin was the only patient.

Nobody could agree on exactly what was wrong with him. But it was plain to see that his mind was not all there.

At the moment, he was sitting on top of his bed in a white hospital gown. His arms were curled around his knees and his eyes were glazed, staring into space. Only the swaying of his body, as if it were being rocked by an invisible force, showed he was alive.

Mulder and Scully watched him through an observation window. For a day they had been waiting for him to come out of his trance and tell them something.

Scully looked at McAlpin's medical chart in the feeble hope she might spot something she had not noticed before.

"The doctor suspects that Private McAlpin suffered a severe concussion during the crash," she said. "It could have caused amnesia—a total loss of memory."

"That would seem possible," Mulder said, nodding. "But that isn't the key question. What interests me is how he came back to life."

Scully shrugged. "It's obvious that he never left. Captain Foyle made a gross error as a doctor when he signed the death certificate."

"You really think that's the case?" Mulder asked, raising his eyebrows.

"It would not be the first time in medical history such a thing has happened," Scully said. "Doctors make mistakes. They're only human."

"And Private McAlpin—is he? Human, I

mean?" Mulder asked, peering again at the swaying hulk on the bed.

"He has all the vital signs of being one of the living," Scully said. "Heartbeat, temperature—everything's normal."

"Do you have the results of his blood test?" Mulder wanted to know.

"Yes." Scully found the paper the lab had sent her and scanned it. "Everything is fine—electrolytes, red and white blood cell count." Then she paused. "Except—this is strange—the tests showed very slight traces of tetrodotoxin."

Mulder's eyes lit up.

"Tetrodotoxin," he said. It was not a question. It was more a statement, as if it were something he already knew—or had guessed.

Still, Scully wanted to make clear what she was talking about. In her work with Mulder, fielding medical questions was her job.

"Tetrodotoxin is a poison found in the liver and other organs of puffer fish—a highly prized Japanese delicacy," Scully said. "Not only do Japanese gourmets pay top prices for that fish served raw in restaurants, they sometimes pay with their lives."

"The problem is, I have a feeling that Private McAlpin did not go to sushi bars," Mulder said, smiling.

Scully recognized that smile.

"You have a theory about how tetrodotoxin got into Jack McAlpin's blood," she said.

"What do you know about zombies?" Mulder asked.

Scully sighed. This was going to be the kind of theory she had come to expect from Mulder. "I don't know much," she said. "Just enough to hope that you don't intend to tell Robin McAlpin that she married one."

Scully went on. "But what do *you* know about zombies, Mulder? I take it you've been doing some research."

"It's extraordinary what you can find on the Web," Mulder said. "In 1982, a Harvard scientist named Wade Davis did fieldwork in Haiti investigating zombies. He learned that voodoo priests used a special powder to turn people into the so-called walking dead. He obtained a number of samples of this powder and did a chemical analysis. He found tetrodotoxin in all of them."

"Mulder," said Scully, shaking her head. "You're talking about a very deadly poison."

"Usually, yes," Mulder said. "But in small enough doses, its effects are not as drastic. It will merely cause paralysis, and lower the heartbeat to a point that the victim might appear dead by normal medical measuring standards."

Believing Mulder was sometimes difficult for Scully. His ideas often ventured into realms fearfully foreign to her way of thinking. But though Scully had no problem arguing with Mulder, she never argued with facts.

The most she could say was, "Zombie or not, Jack McAlpin is definitely alive."

"No question about that," Mulder agreed. "Which makes me wonder about the other Marine who supposedly killed himself."

Scully grimaced. "Are you suggesting what I think you are?"

"Do you see any other way to find out the truth?" Mulder asked.

"You win," Scully said. "Grab a shovel and let's go."

Chapter Eleven

It wasn't as easy as grabbing a shovel, of course. Mulder and Scully worked for the law; they had to go by its rules. It took them a day to get clearance from FBI Headquarters, find an understanding federal judge, and get a court order to dig up a grave.

"*Brrr,*" said Scully with a shiver, as she took her first look at the Folkstone Municipal Cemetery. "This place gives new definition to the word *creepy.*"

"It looks like one of those horror films you like to knock," said Mulder. "Even the weather is right out of central casting."

Thick morning fog shrouded the graveyard. Here and there it parted to reveal tombstones of all shapes and sizes on the rolling, badly tended grounds.

"What a forlorn spot to be buried," Scully said, as they started walking among the grave sites. "Especially for Private Gutierrez. Why would they bury him here—so far from his home in Puerto Rico?"

"Colonel Wharton said that there was no military cemetery nearby—and that the private had no next of kin," Mulder replied.

"I wonder where his grave is," Scully said, peering at the names on the stones they passed. "Though I must admit I'm not terribly eager to start digging. I'd hate to open up his coffin and find another—"

That was as far as she got.

First she heard a low, hostile growling.

Then she saw a snarling shape slowly emerging from the fog.

A moment later, she saw it plain—a dog black as death and bred to kill.

"A rottweiler," muttered Mulder. "Someone means business."

Out of the fog behind the dog came a slender man in complete foul-weather gear. Shaggy brown hair poked out from under his black cap. His face was thin and pale, in need of a shave. That face was young, but his eyes were aged by wariness and worry.

He patted the black dog on its head, and the dog's tail wagged. The growling died away.

He looked Mulder and Scully up and down and said, "They beat you to it."

He watched the agents' mouths drop open, and then went on, "You're the FBI, aren't you?"

Mulder pulled out his ID and got his official voice back. "We have the authority to exhume the body of Manuel Gutierrez."

"Right, the Marine," the man said. "I'm Hiram Sampson, groundskeeper here. I went to prepare the dig as soon as I got the judge's order. But it was already too late. The bodysnatchers got here first." There was anger in his voice.

"The bodysnatchers?" Mulder asked.

"You don't believe me?" Sampson grumbled. "Why should you? Nobody else does. They don't want to listen, because they don't want to be bothered. They call me crazy, just because I take my job seriously. They don't care about the dead once the funeral is over."

"We believe you," Scully said soothingly, after exchanging glances with Mulder. "But we'd like to see for ourselves."

"Come on, then, I'll show you, if you really want to see," Sampson said.

He saw Scully and Mulder looking around them as they moved among the tombstones.

"Sorry the place doesn't look any better," Sampson said. "But I'm the only one here to tend it. Too much for one man, no matter how hard I work, and they don't give me any help."

"These bodysnatchers," said Scully. "Are they a serious problem?"

"I've caught a few of them right in the act," Sampson said. "I chased them away, but they keep coming back, more and more of them, ever since that refugee camp filled up. I can't keep up anymore. That's why I got this."

Sampson parted his coat to show a holstered pistol on his frayed brown belt.

"Don't the police help?" Scully asked.

Sampson gave a short bitter laugh. "They've

got their hands full enough trying to protect the living," he said. "I'm all these folks here got to preserve their rest."

"The bodysnatchers—what do they do with the bodies?" asked Mulder.

"Sell them," Sampson said.

"To whom?" Mulder asked.

"It varies," Sampson said. "A while ago, it was mostly to the local medical school when it ran short of cadavers. Rumor was, the going price was two hundred bucks. Now, though, most of the corpses go to the camp. It's the voodoo types who do the buying."

"Voodoo types?" Scully asked.

"You know, all that native hocus-pocus," Sampson went on. "Not only the refugees, either. Lots of folks in these parts are into that kind of thing. Love potions, medicines, you name what you want done and they think there's some kind of weird magic that can do it."

Then he said, "Here we are."

He stopped at the edge of a large hole half

filled with rainwater. Aside from that, it was empty.

"I don't care what they do with the chickens and pigs," Sampson said. "But this is a sin."

Mulder squatted down to read the small and simple stone that lay on its side at the head of the open grave.

It read, MANUEL GUTIERREZ.

Mulder started to brush away the dirt that hid the dates of birth and death when Scully suddenly exclaimed, "Mulder!"

Straightening up in a flash, he followed Scully's gaze.

In the nearby brush a figure was crouched over, digging away at the ground.

"See what I'm dealing with?" said Sampson, reaching for his gun.

Mulder put his hand on the groundskeeper's gun arm.

"We'll take care of this," he said, and he and Scully were off and running.

The crouched figure saw them too late.

By that time Mulder and Scully had seen who it was—the kid who had sold Mulder the charm in the camp.

All the kid had time to do was drop his trowel and take a few running steps away before Mulder caught up with him and grabbed his arm.

For a minute the boy struggled fiercely, then gave up.

"Let me be," he protested angrily. "I didn't do nothing. What do you want with me?"

"Maybe you can tell us," Mulder said, and pointed to the bulging sack that the boy had left on the ground.

But before the boy could answer, Mulder stiffened.

Beside him, Scully stiffened, too.

Eyes bulging, they both saw the sack begin to move.

Chapter Twelve

As Mulder and Scully watched in horror, inhuman sounds came from the sack.

"Croak . . . croak . . . croak . . . croak."

Then something emerged.

One toad. Then another. Then another.

Ten came out before the sack was empty.

Mulder had to keep a firm hold on the boy's arms to prevent him from going after them.

Meanwhile Scully gave a relieved sigh, and joked, "Maybe I should kiss a few. Find out if one of them is Private Gutierrez."

"I believe we can find out more from this young man," Mulder said, looking into the kid's defiant eyes. "Why don't you tell us exactly what you were doing here."

The boy's lips stayed pressed together. He

was not yielding an inch. For a thin little kid, he managed to stand pretty tall.

"It's against bureau policy to offer you money to talk," Mulder said. "And I don't believe we can offer you any toads to replace the ones you lost. But do you think a super-burger and as many fries as you can hold might get you to cooperate?"

The boy considered the proposition. His mouth opened just wide enough for him to lick his lips. He nodded.

The boy took his time talking, though. First they had to drive to the finest fast food restaurant in Folkstone, which also happened to be the only one. Then the boy wolfed down his burger and fries without taking a deep breath. It was only when he was halfway through his second box of fries that he slowed his munching enough to speak.

"Some people go to that place to dig up bones," he said. "They pay good. But none of that stuff for me. Sick is what I call it. I just go there for the toads. You get the best toads in the graveyard. Don't know why, but you do."

"How do you get out of the camp?" asked Scully, who was sitting beside Mulder across the greasy Formica tabletop from the boy.

The boy stuffed some more fries into his mouth, chomped them down, and said with a shrug, "I go. Then I come back."

"What about your parents?" Scully asked. "Are they at the camp?"

Wordlessly the boy shook his head. Then he turned his attention to some ketchup left in the cardboard container. He dipped in his finger, then licked his finger clean. Next he picked up his jumbo chocolate shake and finished it off.

"How about giving us your name?" Mulder said.

"Chester Bonaparte," the boy said, after his tongue had finished removing the last of the shake from around his mouth.

"What do you do with the toads, Chester?"

"Every one I catch, I get fifty cents," Chester said with the pride of a natural-born businessman.

"Who do you get the money from?" Mulder

asked. "Who do you sell them to?"

Chester leaned forward, as if to reveal an important secret.

Mulder and Scully leaned forward as well, to catch it.

"Bauvais," Chester whispered. "His magic, it is the most strong."

Then Chester's face broke into a big smile. He pointed to the box in front of him and declared, "He even make my french fries disappear."

Chester turned over the empty box and shook it to prove his point. Mulder sighed and pulled out a couple of dollars.

"More fries, more information, right?" he said.

Chester smiled and grabbed the bills.

As Chester headed toward the counter for a refill, Scully told Mulder, "Certain toad species produce a substance called bufotoxin. It bears a close resemblance to tetrodotoxin. It is possible that it was the substance we found in Private McAlpin's blood."

Mulder nodded, but his nod seemed almost absentminded.

Scully raised her voice to press her point. "I think we should ask Bauvais what he does with those toads."

But Mulder only turned his head and peered out the window of the restaurant.

"I think that first we should find out who's following us," he declared. "I didn't say anything before, because I wasn't sure. But I am now. Look out at the parking lot. The gray two-door in the far corner."

Scully glanced through the window as she pretended to reach for sugar for her coffee. "I see it."

"It was behind us when we left the cemetery," Mulder said. "At least that's when I first spotted it. But it could have been on our tail ever since we set out this morning. The fog was so thick, it's hard to say for sure."

"Who could it be?" Scully wondered.

"It's easy enough to find out," said Mulder, getting to his feet. "Keep an eye on Chester while I'm gone."

Mulder casually sauntered to the men's room on the other side of the restaurant. As he had hoped, the rest room had a window looking out toward the rear.

He raised the window and slipped out. Swiftly he moved around the far side of the building. Turning the corner to the parking lot, he made a dash for the cover of a nearby pickup. Creeping from car to car, he made his way closer to the gray two-door.

For a second he crouched behind a red Chevy that was parked beside the gray car.

Then he dashed for the gray car and pulled open the driver's door.

The man behind the wheel almost jumped out of his seat in shock.

"Step out of the car, Private Dunham," Mulder said. "I have a few questions."

Chapter Thirteen

The last time Mulder had seen Private Dunham, the young Marine had been in uniform. At that time, Dunham had let his fear show only in his eyes.

Now, climbing out of his car in civilian clothes, Dunham had fright written all over his face.

He looked even more scared when Mulder glared at him accusingly and said, "You've been following me."

Dunham could barely choke out his answer. "I had to warn you."

"You didn't seem too interested in helping us before," Mulder said, his voice hard as nails.

"I couldn't talk then," Dunham said. "Not

with Colonel Wharton around. He has ears everywhere."

There was a sound of a car door opening nearby.

Dunham froze as if it were a rifle shot.

"And not with *him* right there," Dunham said, pointing behind Mulder.

Mulder turned to see that Scully and Chester had come out of the restaurant and gone to their car. Chester slid into the backseat, and Scully closed the door behind him.

"*Him?*" Mulder asked Dunham.

"Yeah, him."

"Chester?" Mulder asked again. "He's just a little boy."

"No, sir," Dunham said. "He is not."

Before Mulder could pose his next question, Scully came to join them.

"What's going on?" she asked.

"Private Dunham was about to tell us why we're in danger," Mulder said.

"You're putting yourselves in the middle of something you don't understand," Dunham said, his voice urgent.

"But you do," said Mulder.

"*Bauvais warned him!*" Dunham suddenly blurted out.

"Warned who?" Mulder asked. "About what?"

"He warned Colonel Wharton," said Dunham. "Bauvais told him he'd take Wharton's men one by one, unless—"

He stopped, grimacing. It was as if every word, every memory, hurt.

"Unless what?" Mulder demanded.

"Unless the colonel let his people go back to Haiti," Dunham said, painfully forcing the words out. "But the colonel, he just had us turn up the heat."

"The heat? What heat?" Scully wanted to know.

"You know, the beatings and all," Dunham replied, not looking at her.

"Colonel Wharton allowed the beating of refugees?" asked Scully.

"Allowed it? He ordered it," Dunham told her. "That, and worse. What he's making us do to those people—" Dunham could bring himself to say no more. He just shook his head.

"Why hasn't anyone stepped forward and filed a protest?" Scully demanded.

"None of us feel too good about it," Dunham said. "But you don't join the Marines to feel good. You join to do your duty. Doing your duty means following orders."

"Not if they're illegal," Scully said. "The military code clearly states that."

"You don't read law books in boot camp, ma'am," Dunham said. "You learn to do what you're told—and you learn what happens if you don't."

Mulder stepped in to get the questioning back on track. "You said Bauvais threatened to take the colonel's men."

"Bauvais said . . . he'd take their souls," Dunham explained.

"And you believed him," Mulder said.

"Jack McAlpin was my best friend—and look what happened to him," Dunham pointed out.

"We're not sure exactly what happened,"

Scully said firmly. "But there is a medical explanation for his condition."

Dunham looked her in the eye. He shook his head. It wasn't that he was arguing. It was more a sign of sadness.

"I'm sure there must be some medical explanation, ma'am," he said. "And I don't blame you one bit for not believing me. You don't come from New Orleans. You ain't *seen*. You don't *know*."

"Seen what?" Scully asked. "Know what?"

"Back home, a friend of my daddy's, Clyde Jessamin, once crossed a man in some kind of real estate deal," Dunham said. "Not two weeks passed before Jessamin's daughter took ill. The doctors, they couldn't make heads or tails of what was ailing her. All they could do was give her tons of painkillers, she was hurting so bad."

Dunham paused, swallowed, and went on. "She died five minutes past midnight—on what was supposed to be her wedding day. And when the doctors did an autopsy to try to figure it out, guess what they found, ma'am?"

"You tell me, private," Scully said.

"What they found was a bunch of snakes—squirming around in her belly," Dunham told her.

"That sounds like an old wives' tale," Scully declared.

Dunham just shook his head again sadly and said, "No, ma'am, it's not. See, I'm the one who was supposed to marry her."

Chapter Fourteen

Scully didn't know what to say in response to Dunham's story. She was still searching for words as the private got back into his car.

She watched him start the car with a roar of the engine and then speed away with a screech of the tires.

Only then did Scully find her voice.

"You don't actually think he's telling the truth, do you?" she asked Mulder.

"Until I have a reason why Private Dunham might lie, I have to suspend judgment," Mulder answered.

"I'm not saying he's lying," Scully said. "He well may believe what he's saying. He's superstitious, and superstition breeds fear. In turn, that fear breeds even more superstition. That's what voodoo is all about. Voodoo fills people with enough fear to make them see and believe almost anything. But at the bottom it's just as silly as not stepping on cracks in the sidewalk."

"Perhaps," said Mulder. "But there is no doubt that the guy is frightened—very frightened. He even seemed scared of Chester."

"Chester could be working for the colonel," Scully said. "The boy seems willing to do most anything if the price is right."

"But Bauvais seems to trust him, according to Chester," Mulder said. "And Bauvais and the colonel aren't exactly buddies."

Scully nodded. "We do know that Bauvais has someone supplying him with information from the outside world," she said.

"Perhaps toads aren't the only things that Chester sells him," Mulder finished the thought.

"On the other hand, the boy might be spying on Bauvais for the colonel," said Scully.

"Or spying on the colonel for Bauvais."

"We can try to find out from Chester," said Scully, heading back toward their car.

"I'm sure that for another superburger, he'd be happy to tell us something. Whether it would be the truth or not, I'm not prepared to say."

"Uh-oh," said Mulder. The rear door of the car was half open, and an empty paper plate lay on the asphalt beside the car.

Scully swung the door all the way open and looked inside.

The backseat was empty.

"Why would he run away?" she asked. "Think he was afraid of Dunham?"

"Dunham seemed to be the one afraid of him," Mulder said.

"Was he afraid of us, then?" Scully wondered.

"More likely he was afraid of the questions we might ask him after we spoke to Dunham," said Mulder. "Questions we'll definitely have to ask him now."

"First we have to find him," Scully said. "Do you think he headed back to the camp?"

"Not likely. It would be the first place we'd look."

"Which means he could be just about any-where," said Scully.

Mulder and Scully drove up to the Folkstone waterfront.

They faced a maze of brick warehouses, with narrow alleyways between the buildings. Piles of crates were everywhere. A kid the size of Chester could be crouched unseen any-where.

Then they saw him.

Chester saw them, too. Moving quickly, his oversize combat vest flapping, he darted into an alley.

Mulder jumped out of the car. "Drive around the building and try to cut him off at the other end," he said to Scully through the open window. Then he raced into the alley after Chester.

Far ahead of him, he saw the boy's fleeing figure.

"Chester!" Mulder shouted. "Stop! We have to talk!"

In response, Chester made a sharp right turn into another alley.

Mulder ran after him, feet pounding.

"You don't have to run!" Mulder called out, gaining on him. "We're not here to hurt you!"

Chester only ran faster. Mulder, though, kept closing the gap. The boy was only a few feet out of reach when they both tore out of the alleyway into the daylight.

Chester cut sharply around a stack of shipping crates with Mulder right behind.

Then Mulder stopped short.

On the other side of the crates a long pier jutted into Folkstone Harbor.

It was the only place that Chester could have gone.

But it was empty.

The only sign of life came from the seagulls flapping into the air.

Then Mulder heard a hissing sound from above his head.

Glaring down at him from the top of a pier support were the yellow eyes of a huge black cat.

Meowing angrily, it leaped down. In a flash,

it streaked past him, around the crates, and out of sight.

A moment later, Scully drove up.

"Catch up with him?" she asked.

"I'm not sure," Mulder answered.

Chapter Fifteen

Colonel Wharton was a big man, his days were long, and his breakfasts were huge.

This morning he sat at his desk and looked with satisfaction at his breakfast tray. The food was steaming hot. A private named Kittel had brought it to him on the double from the mess hall. Crowding a large platter were a mountain of scrambled eggs, a thick ham steak, and a stack of toast dripping with butter. Beside it was a mammoth mug of coffee loaded with sugar and cream.

Kittel, a tall, lean African American, stood stiffly at attention.

"Can I get you anything else, sir?" he asked.

Colonel Wharton was about to say no and dig into his chow when he heard a sharp knocking.

"Just the door," he said.

Private Kittel opened it, and Mulder and Scully came in.

The sight of the two of them took away Wharton's appetite. Federal snoops like them turned his stomach.

"You can go now," Colonel Wharton told Kittel. After the private had left, Wharton looked at his visitors coldly.

"I was just about to eat breakfast," he said in an icy voice.

"Go right ahead," Mulder said cheerfully. "We already ate."

Wharton scowled. "I understand you obtained a court order to exhume Private Gutierrez," he said angrily.

"That's right," Mulder said.

"Private Gutierrez was a United States Marine," Wharton said. "His corpse should be treated with respect. You should know that I've filed a complaint with the Justice Department."

"I appreciate your concern for the welfare of your men—the dead as well as the living,"

Mulder said. "That's why I think it will interest you to know that the body was missing. Apparently stolen from its grave."

Wharton rose to his feet. His face was flushed.

"I hope you can see now what I'm facing in this camp—and why I have to impose such strict discipline," he said. "What kind of religion would disturb a grave? What kind of people would follow such a faith? These Haitians understand just one thing: primitive force."

"We suspect the incident may be an act of revenge," said Scully, unmoved.

"Revenge?" the colonel responded.

"For your mistreatment of the people in the camp," Scully stated.

"What are you talking about?" he demanded.

"Physical abuse of political refugees is a crime under international law," Scully informed him. "Anyone administering a beating to a refugee or ordering that it be done can be tried in court."

Colonel Wharton curled his lip in disgust.

"It's Bauvais, isn't it?" he asked. "He's the one who has filled your head with all this nonsense. You'd rather believe a foreign rabble-rouser like him than an officer of the United States Marines."

"It is our job to weigh all available evidence," Scully told him.

"Look." Wharton's tone was milder. "Nobody ever said this was a hotel. But it's no concentration camp. We do the best we can with what we have—which is painfully little. As you have seen, we lack proper housing for these people, we lack cooking facilities, we lack recreational space, and we're short-handed to boot. They're crowded in here like animals, and we're stretched thin trying to keep them in line."

"Then there is no official policy of physically harassing the refugees?" Scully asked. "No beatings, no torture, or any other forms of abuse?"

"If anything, it's my men who are being harassed," Colonel Wharton replied. "The refugees may have some reason to be angry—but it is my men who are the innocent victims of that anger. The UN, the relief organizations, all the do-gooders—they're busy protecting the rights of the refugees. But no one looks out for my men."

Mulder nodded. Scully looked at her partner, slightly surprised. "I can see your point," he said. "Well, thank you for your time. We'll let you finish your breakfast before it gets cold."

Scully started to open her mouth, but Mulder silenced her with a look.

"Have a good day, Colonel," he said, and held the door for Scully. He followed her out of the office, closing the door behind him.

Glowering, Wharton stared at the door. Then he turned back to his breakfast, his stomach rumbling ravenously.

Licking his lips, he speared his fork into his thick ham steak. His knife sliced into the pink meat.

Then he let go of both his knife and his fork.

His watering mouth went dry.

He saw red.

Red blood.

The blood gushed out of the cut in the ham.

It flowed over the edge of the plate.

It streamed across the desktop toward him.

Before it could hit his lap, he pushed back his chair and stood up.

Colonel Wharton had lost his appetite for the most important meal of the day.

Chapter Sixteen

"The colonel has clearly told us all that he's going to," Mulder said as he and Scully walked away from Wharton's office.

"But he's sandbagging us," Scully protested.

"Soldiers use sandbags to protect their positions," Mulder said. "We have to find a way to get through his defenses."

"I wonder what makes him despise the people here so much," Scully said.

"Perhaps it's for making him do a job he hates," Mulder said. "Colonel Wharton doesn't feel that he and his men should be used as prison guards."

"Perhaps," said Scully. "But I don't think that explains his hostility. It's too intense."

"I've learned that the colonel commanded

this Marine detachment when they went to Haiti last year," Mulder said. "The job of keeping the peace there must have been difficult. Especially for an officer much more at ease in waging war. He well might have developed a hearty dislike of the people he was supposed to protect. Especially if they refused to be grateful for that protection. The Haitians may have needed help from us. But nobody likes foreigners coming in and taking charge of their affairs for even the best of reasons."

By now Mulder and Scully were crossing the crowded prison yard on the way to their car. The eyes of the refugees followed them— giving them looks dark as a storm about to break.

"*Brrr,*" said Scully, as a Marine guard let them out. "You can feel those people's rage. I can't say I blame them. Caged in here like animals—in what they thought would be the land of the free."

Scully got behind the wheel of their car, and Mulder slid in beside her.

He glanced at the refugees crowded inside

the fence, faces against the chain link, eyes still darkly glowering.

"The way I see it," he said, "Wharton has left them with no choice but to fight back with the only weapon they have."

"I'm sorry, Mulder," Scully said. "But there's a big difference between angry looks and raising the dead to exact revenge on the living."

"Not according to Private Dunham," Mulder replied.

"I think Private Dunham heard too many New Orleans folktales when he was a child," said Scully. She took the car key out and asked, "Where to now? Any more graveyards in town?"

But before Mulder could answer, Scully cried, "*Ow*!"

She jerked her hand back, leaving the key in the ignition.

She looked at her palm, and Mulder followed her eyes.

A drop of blood welled out from her skin.

"What happened?" Mulder asked.

"This," Scully said.

She pointed to a thorny vine wrapped around the steering column. "More scare tactics."

"We'll have to be more alert," said Mulder.

"More importantly, we have to show those people that scare tactics don't work," Scully said. She looked out through the open car window at the faces still watching them through the fence.

Carefully she freed the vine and tossed it out the window.

Meanwhile Mulder was looking at her with concern.

"Let me take a look at the wound," he said.

"It's nothing," Scully declared, and turned the key in the ignition. The engine came to life.

"Let's get this show on the road," Scully said briskly. Her hand did throb a bit. But she was not about to admit it. Scully did not believe in letting weakness show. Not in front of Mulder. Not in front of anyone, not even herself.

She resisted the impulse to check her hand. And she refused to give another glance to where the vine of thorns lay outside the car door.

Neither she nor Mulder saw the symbol chalked on the asphalt there.

The same symbol as on the tree that Private McAlpin had crashed his car into.

The same symbol as on the stool from which Private Gutierrez had jumped with a noose around his neck.

The same symbol that McAlpin's little boy had found in his sandbox and McAlpin's wife had stared at in horror.

The symbol that Pierre Bauvais had called the *loco-miroir*—the crossroads between the world of the living and the world of the dead.

Had Scully looked, she might have wondered what road she was on right now.

But she did not, as she sped straight ahead.

Meanwhile, in his isolation cell, Pierre Bauvais, too, fought against showing weakness.

He had a harder job doing it than Scully.

His pain was far more intense.

For fifteen minutes Private Kittel had been using him as a punching bag.

Kittel's face was beaded with sweat from his violent efforts.

Bauvais's face was bleeding and swollen.

But his puffed-up eyes refused to blink.

His split lips were firmly pressed together.

Finally, panting, Private Kittel stepped aside, and Colonel Wharton took his place.

"I don't think he's in any condition to talk, sir," Kittel reported, standing at stiff attention.

"That's right, Private," the colonel snapped. "You don't think. You follow orders."

"Yes sir," Kittel said, choking the words out.

"And your order is, you keep your mouth shut about this—especially to outsiders," Wharton said. "What happens in our detachment stays in our detachment."

"Yes sir," Kittel answered. "But sir—"

That was as far as he got.

"You're dismissed," the colonel barked.

"Yes sir," the private said. He gave a sharp

salute, turned on his heel, and left the cell. The door clanged shut behind him, echoing.

As the echoes died, Wharton leaned forward toward Bauvais, who sat on the edge of his bunk, still groggy from the blows.

"Now, tell me," Wharton whispered harshly.

Bauvais kept his lips closed.

"*Ouvri barrier pou' moi*," Wharton demanded in Haitian Creole. Then he went back to his natural language of command. "Give me the secret."

Bauvais stayed silent. Only his eyes declared his defiance.

Wharton's mouth curved in a sneer.

"I suggest you tell me while you can still talk," he told Bauvais.

Finally Bauvais answered.

"*Ma vie dans mains Bon Dieu*," he declared. To make sure the colonel understood, he said, "My life is in the hands of the Good Lord."

"No, *Papaloi*," Wharton said, in a voice as brutally punishing as Private Kittel's fists. "Your life is in *my* hands."

Chapter Seventeen

Mulder and Scully drove back to their motel. Before they went to their separate rooms, they split up the work to be done.

"I think I should be the one to question Private Dunham further," Scully said. "I know you do your best to stay detached, Mulder. But you do lean in a certain direction. And you have been known to be swayed when a lead seems to head that way."

Mulder smiled. "Private Dunham is yours, Scully. I'll see what I can find out about Colonel Wharton's record as a commander," he added as he headed toward his room.

When Mulder opened the door to his room, his plans suddenly changed.

A playing card fluttered to his feet from

where it had been stuck in the upper edge of the door.

The inside upper edge.

Mulder wasn't surprised that the man who had left the card there had been able to gain entry to the room.

That man seemed to have keys to everything—including the most closely guarded secrets of the government. He had better access to them than even the bloodhounds at *The Lone Gunman*. And some of the tidbits he chose to give Mulder went beyond their wildest nightmares.

The playing card was the calling card of the man called X.

Mulder looked at the card.

It was the ten of diamonds.

It was no accident X used playing cards to announce himself. X liked to play games. Mulder would have to gamble that he could figure out what the ten of diamonds meant.

Mulder could be sure of only one thing. He would have to wait until night to find out if his gamble paid off.

At ten that night, Mulder's headlights lit up the diamond-shaped county road marker: "10."

He pulled his car to the side of the deserted highway. He shut off his lights, and waited.

He did not have to wait long.

He saw headlights up the road. A dark sedan was coming toward him. It stopped two feet from his parked car, the headlights flooding over him. Then the lights went out.

His eyes still blurred, Mulder saw a dark shape come out of the sedan. Mulder's passenger door swung open, and a man slid in beside him.

Mulder knew better than to turn his head. Even when Mulder gave a quick sidelong glance, X looked annoyed.

Mulder, though, was not there to look. He was there to listen.

"Why are you here?" he asked.

"To tell you that your investigation has failed," X said.

"But we have a loose-cannon colonel who

is violating every human rights law on the books," Mulder protested.

"In twenty-four hours, the military will declare the Folkstone camp off limits to outsiders. That means the press, social agencies, and all independent observers."

"And Scully and me?" asked Mulder.

"You will be assigned another case—supposedly more important," X informed him.

"They're making the camp invisible," said Mulder. "But why?"

"In case you haven't noticed, the Statue of Liberty is on vacation. Her message 'Give me your tired, your poor . . . the wretched refuse of your teeming shore' is in the dead-letter file. Her lamp is out—the fuel bill was too high."

"And who's taken her place?" Mulder asked.

"We have a new greeting for people who show up at our shining gate," X stated. "It's written in sky-high letters. 'If you're not a citizen, keep out!'"

"But these people are already here," Mulder said.

"We'd rather not know about it," X replied. "Out of sight, out of mind."

"Okay, point taken," said Mulder. "But then why keep the Haitians locked up here? They want to go back to Haiti now. Why not just let them?"

"They will be allowed to go back—in time," X answered. "But first Colonel Wharton has a lesson to teach them. It seems that when our troops were in Haiti last year, three of his men took their own lives. Two of them were under the colonel's direct command. For the colonel, it's payback time."

"You mean the military is approving of the colonel taking revenge on innocent civilians?" Mulder asked. "There are people in Congress who might have a problem with that—when I inform them."

Out of the corner of his eye, Mulder saw X give him a smile. It was a smile of pity for Mulder's innocence. Or ignorance. Or both.

"By the time they get their act together and begin an official inquiry, the camp will be nothing but empty warehouses again," X stated. "It will be as if nothing had ever happened here."

Mulder tried to think of a reply.

But X didn't give him a chance. He slid out of the car, returned to his sedan, and drove away.

Mulder was left sitting alone in the dark, searching for some ray of hope, and seeing only a torch that had been snuffed out.

Chapter Eighteen

Scully had a telephone receiver cradled between her shoulder and her ear.

She was listening to white noise over it.

It was driving her crazy.

"Hello . . . hello," she shouted at whoever was on the other end—if there *was* anyone there.

"Yes, ma'am," a bored voice finally answered.

"Look, I've been on hold for half an hour," she said.

"Sorry, ma'am," the voice said. "I've just come on shift. Guy here before me, guess he forgot to tell me you were there. What can I do for you?"

"I'm trying to contact Private Harry Dunham," Scully said as calmly as she could.

"Dunham?" the voice said. "Let me check the duty roster."

A moment later, the voice reported, "Private Dunham is off duty."

"Perhaps he's in the barracks," Scully suggested.

"I'll put you on hold and give the barracks a ring," the voice said.

Before Scully could say another word, she was listening to white noise again.

Foot tapping, she absentmindedly scratched the palm of her hand. It was itching. Then she felt a stab of pain. She looked at her palm, and her whole body stiffened.

The wound from the thorny vine in the car had not gotten better. The antibiotic ointment she had put on it had not helped.

In fact, it had gotten worse. The skin around it was red and puckered. And blood had begun to ooze from it.

Grimacing, Scully looked away—and caught sight of herself in the motel room mirror. Her face was white and puffy. *I don't look well*, she thought, and even as she thought it, her face began to blur.

Her head was pounding now, like a drum beating harder and harder.

The voice on the phone broke the beat.

"Sorry, ma'am, Private Dunham is not in the barracks. And nobody there knows where he is."

Scully pulled herself together. She'd have to put some more ointment on the wound. Later she'd take a hot bath and get some shut-eye to get rid of whatever bug she had. But she had some work to do first.

"Thank you," she said, and hung up.

She left her room and went down the motel corridor to a room at the far end.

She knocked on the door.

There was no response.

"Mulder," she said loudly through the door. "I finally got through to the camp, and Dunham's not there."

Still there was no answer.

"Funny," she said under her breath, and tried the door.

The knob turned, and the door swung open.

She entered the room, saying, "Mulder, your door's unlocked."

Then she realized the room was empty.

From the bathroom she heard the sound of running water.

She went to the closed bathroom door and knocked on it. "Mulder," she called out over the sound of the water.

Then she felt something against her shoe.

She looked down and saw water flowing out from under the bathroom door.

The water was pink.

But not pretty pink.

Bloody pink.

The water flooded out when Scully flung open the door.

She saw it pouring out from over the side of the bathtub. She splashed across the white tile floor and turned off the gushing faucet.

Then she stared at the clothed body in the tub.

She could see his face dipping below the waterline.

She could see blood coming out of his chest through a gaping rip in his shirt.

She no longer had to wonder where Private Harry Dunham was.

She had no time to wonder anything else before she heard the sound of heavy footsteps.

She wheeled around to see a massive man in combat fatigues framed in the doorway. She recognized him instantly.

There was blood on Private McAlpin's face and beneath his chin. There was more blood on his shirt and on his hands. But it was not his blood.

His eyes were open—but they stared at her sightlessly.

His huge hands flexed and unflexed as he came toward her.

Scully's heart may not have stopped. But it felt as if it did.

Then it started pounding double time as the big Marine lurched forward—after Mulder gave him a hard shove from behind.

In Mulder's other hand was a gun pointed straight at McAlpin's head.

"Are you okay?" Mulder asked, keeping his gun fixed on McAlpin. "I was worried there for a second. I thought—"

"I'm fine," Scully said. "It's Dunham."

She pointed to the tub.

McAlpin reacted before Mulder did. The Marine stumbled toward the tub like a sleepwalker starting to wake. He stared down at the corpse with glassy eyes slowly clearing. His frozen face began to melt in pain.

Mulder kept him covered with his gun.

With his other hand, Mulder pulled a long object wrapped in a newspaper from his jacket pocket.

He handed it to Scully.

As she unwrapped it, he told her, "I found him wandering outside. He was holding that."

Scully looked down at a knife. Its wooden handle was carved in the form of a snake ready to strike. The blood on its double-edged blade showed that it had.

Chapter Nineteen

The room for questioning prisoners was not much different from the wire mesh isolation cells in the camp basement. But instead of a bunk, it had a long table with benches for the prisoner and those quizzing him.

Private Jack McAlpin sat on one side of the table now, Mulder and Scully on the other.

Colonel Wharton stood a few feet away, like a massive statue watching over the scene.

"You don't recall leaving the hospital?" Mulder asked McAlpin.

The private rubbed the heel of his hand over his forehead, trying to remember.

His eyes looked like those of a stunned boxer, who had taken one too many punches.

Slowly he shook his head.

"All I remember," he said haltingly, "is

being there . . . seeing him . . . seeing all that blood . . ."

"Then why did you sign a confession saying that you murdered him?" Scully asked.

McAlpin's mouth hung open, but no words came out. His eyes begged for someone to supply them.

Colonel Wharton answered by stepping forward and saying, "Private McAlpin asked me about the crime. I simply gave him the facts."

"The facts?" Scully asked.

"The fact of the brutal murder," Wharton said. "That fact that Private McAlpin was found nearby with blood on his face and clothes, and with a bloody knife in his hand. The fact that the blood matched the blood of the victim."

McAlpin bowed his head in guilt and shame. "Who else but me could have done it?" he replied.

Mulder looked at him, then turned to Wharton. "Colonel, could we have a word in private outside?" he asked coldly.

"Of course, Agent Mulder," Wharton said easily.

Mulder and Scully followed the colonel past the guard at the door and out into the corridor.

When the three were alone, Mulder demanded, "What exactly did you say to him? And what did you do to him?"

"I hope you are not suggesting I forced Private McAlpin into anything against his will," the colonel said.

"I simply want to make sure that it was his own idea to sign the confession," Mulder said.

"Of course it was," Wharton assured him. "And you will have a very difficult time trying to prove otherwise."

Mulder gave Wharton an icy look. But he could do nothing to rub away the colonel's smug smile.

Meanwhile Scully looked down at her palm, which was itching more and more. Scratching it didn't relieve the itch, but for the moment it was the best she could do.

"Now if you have no other questions . . ." said the colonel.

"But we do," Mulder said. "Since Private McAlpin returned to the land of the living, has he had any contact with Pierre Bauvais?"

"Not to my knowledge," Wharton said.

"Still, we would like to speak to Bauvais to find out for sure."

Wharton shrugged. "I'm afraid that's not possible."

"Why not?" Mulder asked. "As agents of the Federal Bureau of Investigation, we have the power to demand your cooperation."

"I'm quite aware of that," Wharton said, unruffled. "But you still can't talk to Bauvais—unless you have powers I am unaware of."

"What do you mean?" Mulder asked.

"He's dead," Wharton said. His voice was casual, without a trace of emotion. He might have been talking about the weather. "Last night Bauvais cut his wrists with a bedspring."

Mulder stared at him in shock.

Scully was just as shocked, her itching palm forgotten.

Colonel Wharton savored their reaction for a long moment. Then he told them, "I'll have a copy of the suicide report sent to your motel. I'll send a copy of Private McAlpin's confession along with it. I think you'll find everything in order, and that your business here is finished."

Before he turned to go, the colonel added, "I wish you luck on your next assignment. I trust it will prove more rewarding than this one."

With that, Colonel Wharton went back into the room where Private McAlpin waited.

Scully winced at the clang as the colonel slammed the metal door behind him.

The noise made her head begin to hurt again. The drumbeat inside her skull resumed. She rubbed her forehead with two fingers to quiet the pounding.

"What's wrong?" Mulder asked.

"Nothing," Scully said, quickly dropping her hand to her side. "Just a little headache.

This case does have a certain amount of stress."

But Mulder kept looking at her hard.

"This headache—when did it start?" he asked.

"I tell you, it's nothing," Scully insisted.

"That scratch on your palm—could I have a look at—?" he began.

But he was interrupted by a buzzing in his jacket pocket.

He pulled out his cell phone.

"Mulder," he said.

He listened, then said, "We'll be right there. Don't let anyone else in."

He snapped the phone off, and told Scully, "It's Robin McAlpin. She's found something interesting—very interesting."

Chapter Twenty

Stop scratching—it'll only make it worse, Scully said to herself. *If only this itching would go away!*

But the itching did not go away. It kept on and on, worse and worse. It took all of Scully's willpower to keep her fingernails away from it. It took an effort to get her mind off it and to pay attention to what Robin McAlpin was saying.

Scully sat with Mulder in the McAlpins' living room. Little Luke was taking his nap upstairs. Robin kept her voice low to keep from waking her child. But it was easy to hear how badly she was hurting.

"First I thought I had lost Jack," she said. "Then he came back—but his mind seemed gone. Now they're saying that he killed Harry."

"He said it himself," Scully had to reply. "He signed a confession."

"I don't care," Robin said. "It doesn't make sense. I know my husband. Jack may have been under a strain, but he'd never harm Harry. Harry Dunham was his best friend."

"Mrs. McAlpin," Mulder cut in. "You said on the phone that Private Dunham came here last night."

"Yes."

"For what reason?"

"He was on his way to see you," Robin answered, pulling herself together. She wanted to be of help to the only two people in the world who might help her husband.

"Why did Private Dunham want to see us?" Mulder asked.

"He wouldn't tell me," Robin said. "I've never seen anyone so scared. He said that if anything happened to him, I should give this to you."

She went to a cabinet and unlocked a drawer, then pulled out a sealed manila envelope.

At that moment, the sound of the baby crying came from upstairs.

"Luke's been in a mood ever since all this started," Robin said. "It's like he knows what's going on."

"Children can be extremely sensitive to their surroundings," said Scully.

"Right now I wish it weren't so," Robin said. "Here, you look at this. I'll be right back."

She handed Mulder the envelope. Then she headed upstairs to soothe her child.

The crying stopped a few minutes later. But by that time Mulder and Scully had already stopped hearing it.

They were totally focused on the black-and-white photo Mulder had taken from the envelope.

"Dunham must have known what was going on," Scully said.

"If anyone was tuned in to the truth, it would have been him," Mulder agreed.

The photo showed a ceremony in a jungle clearing. In the foreground were Haitian men dancing and chanting. Behind them, looking on, stood Pierre Bauvais. His arms were partially raised, like those of an orchestra conductor. And behind him, looking over his shoulder, was another familiar face.

"Colonel Wharton," said Scully.

"Out of uniform, but unmistakable," said Mulder.

"So Wharton knew Bauvais in Haiti when he was stationed there," Scully said. She gave the photo another hard look. "Knew him more than casually, it seems. I don't think strangers are invited to voodoo ceremonies."

Mulder shrugged. "When in Rome . . ." he said. He studied the photo a few moments more. "It would seem that Bauvais was in charge of the show. Chester did tell us his magic was most powerful. We can assume that Bauvais was acting here as a *hungan*—a voodoo priest."

"And what would that make the colonel?" Scully wondered. She looked closely at Wharton's face. "He certainly seems interested in the ceremony. More than just a tourist would be. He looks like he wants to drink in every little detail."

"To the last red drop," said Mulder. "I think we can call the colonel a student."

"And his teacher?"

"The man who knew what Wharton wanted to learn," Mulder replied, looking at Bauvais's commanding presence.

"And if Bauvais refused to reveal that knowledge . . ." said Scully, with dawning understanding.

Mulder finished her thought. "The colonel might seek ways to make the teacher teach."

"Still, why would Wharton want the secrets of voodoo so badly?" Scully asked.

"Perhaps leading his Marines wasn't enough for him," Mulder suggested. "Perhaps he wanted to command the army of the dead as well."

Chapter Twenty-one

"That wound on your palm still bothering you?" Mulder asked in a whisper.

Scully realized she had been scratching it without thinking. She stopped at once.

"It's nothing," she said. "It just got irritated climbing over the fence." She looked around her at the empty moonlit courtyard of the Folkstone Processing Center. "It doesn't bother me half as much as *this*. The law would call this trespassing."

"Do you think any judge would give us a search warrant on the suspicion that a U.S. Marine colonel is practicing voodoo?" Mulder asked.

"Not likely," Scully acknowledged.

"Without obtaining hard evidence, do you think we could convince anyone that

Wharton is doing such a thing?" Mulder went on.

"Okay, point taken." Breaking the law to enforce the law went against Scully's grain. But there were times when Mulder and the force of necessity could persuade her to give in.

Mulder left the rope that they had used to climb the camp fence in a coil on the ground. They could use it to go back out after they'd found what they were looking for—if there was anything to find.

Scully followed her partner into the main building. The door was unguarded. *Security here is lax*, she thought. *No wonder that kid, Chester, is able to come and go as he pleases.*

Inside all was quiet. It was three in the morning and everyone was asleep. They tiptoed past the dormitories of the refugees. They went up the stairs in the back, to Colonel Wharton's office.

The door was unlocked. They entered, and Mulder closed the door behind them. Only then did he turn on his flashlight.

Scully went to the desk and turned on the lamp.

"I'll check out the drawers," she said, and opened a lower one.

"Uggh," she said.

"What is it?" asked Mulder, who had gone to a metal trunk he'd spotted in a corner.

Scully held up what she had found.

"What on earth is that?" he asked.

"A severed rooster foot—with its claws sticking into a sheet of paper," Scully replied.

Gingerly she pulled the grisly foot from the paper. Then she smoothed the paper out and read it.

"It's a Marine Corps officer complaint form," Scully told him.

"I take it this one is filled out," Mulder said.

"By privates Gutierrez and Dunham," Scully continued. "They charge Colonel Wharton with human rights abuses. They describe beatings and torture, with names, dates, and places."

Meanwhile Mulder had lifted the lid of the trunk.

He shined his light inside. Then he reached in his hand and pulled out a military-issue dog tag dangling on its chain.

"Anything else in there?" Scully asked.

"Come look," Mulder said.

But before she could, the light of another flashlight flooded the room.

Mulder swung his light around.

Private Kittel blinked in the glare, but kept the big .45 in his other hand steady.

"Get that light out of my eyes," the tall Marine commanded.

Mulder obeyed.

"Come with me, please," Kittel said coldly.

"Where's Colonel Wharton?" Mulder demanded.

"You'll find out soon enough," said Kittel.

"He killed Bauvais," Mulder said. His voice was razor-edged.

Kittel winced, but silently stood his ground.

Mulder pressed harder. "If you know anything about it, you'll be tried as an accessory to murder."

"Shut up!" But he was not giving an order. He was making a plea.

Mulder obeyed. But Kittel could not stand the silence. "Bauvais got what he deserved," he said defiantly. "After what what he did to McAlpin and Gutierrez."

"It wasn't Bauvais," Scully said, looking him in the eye.

"What are you talking about?" Kittel asked, blinking.

"Those men were about to testify against Wharton," Scully said. "He had to stop them before they did."

Mulder stepped in. "If you don't believe us, look in the trunk."

Warily Kittel went to the trunk, his gun still at the ready. He shined his flashlight inside.

His mouth dropped open. His gun arm drooped downward, the weapon forgotten.

Scully went to the trunk and looked into it herself.

What she saw made the rooster claw look pretty.

Inside the trunk was a pile of white bones.

Scully had not gone to medical school for nothing.

She knew human bones when she saw them.

"You're looking at what's left of Private Gutierrez," Mulder told Kittel and handed the private the dog tag.

Kittel read it, and looked sick.

"Now, what happened to Bauvais's body?" Mulder demanded.

Kittel said, his voice weak as water, "They . . . we buried him . . . this afternoon."

"Where?" Mulder wanted to know.

"In the town graveyard," Kittel said.

"Mulder, what does Bauvais's resting place have to do with anything?" Scully asked.

"I believe that where we find Bauvais, we'll find Colonel Wharton," Mulder replied.

"But Bauvais is dead," Scully said. "What would Wharton want with him?"

"Anyone can kill a man," Mulder said. "Wharton wants his soul."

Chapter Twenty-two

In the Folkstone Municipal Cemetery, candles burned in a shroud of fog.

The flames flickered around an open grave.

The gravestone read PIERRE BAUVAIS.

Beside the grave stood the massive figure of Colonel Samuel Wharton.

Tonight he wore no uniform. Instead he wore flowing robes from an island country far away.

The words he spoke came from that island, too. *"Au nom des Saints de la Lune . . . "*

In the name of the Saints of the Moon . . .

Moonlight filtering through the fog shone on him as he worked a winch to raise a coffin from the grave. Sweat poured down his face as he swung the coffin up and out and let it drop to the ground with a thud.

From his robes Wharton pulled a knife—a knife with a wooden handle shaped like a snake about to strike.

He used it to slice open a red velvet pouch.

White power spilled onto the ground from the pouch. Wharton used it to draw a circle on the ground around the coffin. Then he used what was left to complete the symbol of the *loco-miroir* on the cemetery ground. His voice rose in a chant of triumph: "*Au nom des Saints des Etoiles . . .*"

In the name of the Saints of the Stars . . .

This was the night that Wharton had lived for.

This was the night he had killed for.

This was the night that would give him the powers of darkness, make him the king of the night.

Scully, with Mulder beside her, drove as fast as she could. The headlights of the car cut through the fog. Finally gravestones appeared, one after another. Scully braked to a stop, and Mulder jumped out.

Then he stopped. He suddenly realized that Scully was not following him. She was sitting behind the wheel, both hands pressing into her temples.

"What's wrong?" he asked.

Scully forced herself to lower her hands.

"Nothing. Just a flash headache. Too much tension in this case. It'll pass—and I'll be right there."

Still Mulder hestitated. He had never seen Scully's face so pale. She looked like a ghost.

Scully bit her lip, and put strength in her voice. "Don't worry, I'll be fine. Just . . . get Wharton."

She managed to give him a steady look—steady enough to satisfy her partner.

She managed to keep herself together until he headed off into the fog.

Then the pounding in her head grew too intense.

Her mouth opened in a silent groan. But she forgot her pain when she saw her face in the rearview mirror.

Her lips were parted slightly. A pink froth coated them. Eyes wide with horror, she opened her mouth and saw blood welling out from around her gums.

Still staring in the mirror, she felt the itching of her palm grow unbearable.

She looked down and saw that her whole palm had turned red.

Before her eyes, the small wound grew bigger.

It widened to a hole, and blood poured out of it.

Then clear oily liquid began to pour out of the hole.

As Scully watched in horror, one finger poked out of the hole. Then another. And another. And another.

An entire hand was out now.

An arm stretched out behind it as it reached for Scully's throat.

A second hand joined it, followed by the rest of a man whom Scully had seen once but had not forgotten. The big Haitian who had threatened her the first time she had visited the refugee camp.

He was delivering on that threat now, as his two huge hands tightened their choking hold.

Scully screamed for her life.

But the car doors and windows were closed.

And Mulder was out of earshot.

Mulder was moving through the fog, flashlight in one hand, gun in the other.

The fog parted, and he saw the hulking back of a man. The man's bald head was lit by the light of candles. A long knife gleamed in his hand.

Mulder heard the man chanting, *"Au nom de Saint de Tempete . . ."*

In the name of the Saint of the Storm . . .

Mulder leveled his gun and shouted, "Colonel Wharton! Federal agent!"

Wharton turned, and Mulder saw his eyes.

They were the red eyes of a wild creature.

Wharton's voice was the snarl of a beast. *"Voici yun garde protection pou' marche dans la nuit . . ."*

So here's a protector of the law out walking in the night . . .

A shiver ran through Mulder. He stiffened himself against it.

"Put down the knife," he commanded, and raised his gun to firing position.

Wharton's red eyes stared at the gun.

Then slowly he nodded.

He bent and laid the red velvet pouch gently on a toppled gravestone.

Then suddenly he drove the knife into the cloth.

Mulder's gun dropped as he doubled over from the pain slicing through his guts.

Wharton's eyes were cold and clear now as he turned to flee into the night.

But they glazed with shock when a figure dark as night suddenly blocked his path.

Chapter Twenty-three

Pierre Bauvais's clothes were torn and blood-stained. His face was battered and caked with blood. But he stood erect and his eyes were focused like lasers as they burned into Wharton's.

"*Ca quoi fait mal, ce mal li we,*" Bauvais said. His voice seemed to come from far away, beyond the borders of the night.

He who does evil, evil he will see.

Wharton gave an animal grunt, and raised his knife.

Bauvais took a deep breath—and blew a cloud of white powder into Wharton's face.

Wharton dropped his knife and clawed at his burning eyes.

Legs giving way, he fell to the ground, writhing.

Wharton gave a final spasm, then lay still, as Bauvais faded back into the darkness.

Mulder still did not have the strength to rise. But he felt his own pain fading.

And for the first time, noticed that Scully had not followed him.

Scully could no longer scream. The hands around her throat were squeezing too tight. Through the mist of pain, she could just make out the Haitian's dead, unseeing eyes, and the saliva dripping from his mouth. Desperately she squinted beyond him, searching for a weapon.

All she could see was Chester's cloth charm. It dangled from the rearview mirror— just out of reach.

With her last ounce of strength, Scully pushed up against the weight pressing her down. It yielded only inches—but it was enough.

Her hand closed over the charm. She ripped it free as she was shoved backward again.

Then the weight was gone.

The Haitian was gone.

The headache and itching were gone.

So was the wound on her palm.

All that was left was a throbbing in her throat and the cloth charm in her hand.

Shaking her head numbly, Scully stared through the windshield—and met a pair of gleaming yellow eyes.

A large black cat on the car hood me-owed—then leaped off into the night.

Scully took a deep breath, then exhaled. She felt her heartbeat return to normal.

She left the car and headed in the direction Mulder had gone.

Minutes later she saw him, on his hands and knees.

As she hurried to him, he got to his feet shakily, like a running back after a crunching tackle.

"You okay?" he asked Scully anxiously.

"I feel a lot better than you look," she told him.

"At least I'm in better shape than he is," Mulder said, pointing to where Colonel

Wharton lay face down in the dirt.

"What happened?" Scully asked.

"I don't know—not for sure, anyway."

Scully knelt by the body. She checked for a pulse.

"He's dead," she said. She looked up at Mulder. "Did you—?"

"No," Mulder said shortly, in a voice that allowed for no more questions.

Scully nodded, and got up to follow him to where a closed coffin lay beside an open grave.

Slowly Mulder lifted the creaking lid.

Inside lay the body of Pierre Bauvais.

"He seems to have died at peace, for such an angry man," Scully commented. "You could even say he's smiling."

"I guess he found eternal rest at last," Mulder agreed. "I think I can safely close the lid."

Chapter Twenty-four

"Everything all right with you?" Scully asked Private Jack McAlpin.

"I don't even have bad dreams anymore," McAlpin answered with a smile.

"And this bad dream is ending too," said Mulder, as he watched the Haitians filing onto the military transport trucks. They were leaving the processing center, bound for a ship waiting in Folkstone Harbor to take them to Haiti.

"It can't end too soon for them—or for me and my buddies," McAlpin said. "This isn't the kind of job we joined the service to do."

"Do you have the list we requested?" Scully asked.

"Yes, ma'am." McAlpin handed her a thick

binder. "The name of every Haitian going back."

As Scully started skimming the list, McAlpin added, "The Haitians are requesting that Bauvais be returned to Haiti, too."

"Too bad he has to go in a box," Mulder commented.

Meanwhile Scully was going through the list a second time. Her brow was furrowed.

"Is this list complete?" she asked.

"As far as I know," McAlpin replied.

"There's a name missing," Scully said. "A boy. Bonaparte. Chester Bonaparte. You know him?"

"Chester?" McAlpin shook his head in sorrow. "Yeah, I knew him. Great kid. He died six weeks ago in that riot."

Scully and Mulder exchanged looks.

They didn't have to say a word to share what they were thinking.

So much dying in this case.

And so little death.

X X X

Hiram Sampson started the engine on the small bulldozer. Shifting it into gear, he drove forward slowly, pushing the dirt back into the grave that had recently held the body of Pierre Bauvais. But the grave was not empty. Instead, it held a different coffin. A coffin with the body of Colonel Samuel Wharton inside.

Sampson watched through the window as the dirt dropped down into the hole. He could not hear the soft thud of the earth falling onto the coffin. Nor could he hear the pounding of fists or the desperate cries that came from inside the coffin as the dirt piled higher and higher.